Dear Parent:

Congratulations! Your child is taking the first steps on an exciting journey. The destination? Independent reading!

STEP INTO READING® will help your child get there. The program offers five steps to reading success. Each step includes fun stories and colorful art. There are also Step into Reading Sticker Books, Step into Reading Math Readers, Step into Reading Write-In Readers, Step into Reading Phonics Readers, and Step into Reading Phonics First Steps! Boxed Sets—a complete literacy program with something for every child.

Learning to Read, Step by Step!

Ready to Read   Preschool–Kindergarten
• big type and easy words • rhyme and rhythm • picture clues
For children who know the alphabet and are eager to begin reading.

Reading with Help   Preschool–Grade 1
• basic vocabulary • short sentences • simple stories
For children who recognize familiar words and sound out new words with help.

Reading on Your Own   Grades 1–3
• engaging characters • easy-to-follow plots • popular topics
For children who are ready to read on their own.

Reading Paragraphs   Grades 2–3
• challenging vocabulary • short paragraphs • exciting stories
For newly independent readers who read simple sentences with confidence.

Ready for Chapters   Grades 2–4
• chapters • longer paragraphs • full-color art
For children who want to take the plunge into chapter books but still like colorful pictures.

STEP INTO READING® is designed to give every child a successful reading experience. The grade levels are only guides. Children can progress through the steps at their own speed, developing confidence in their reading, no matter what their grade.

Remember, a lifetime love of reading starts with a single step!

Thomas the Tank Engine & Friends
A Britt Allcroft Company Production
Based on The Railway Series by the Rev. W. Awdry
Copyright © 2000 Gullane (Thomas) LLC
All rights reserved under International and Pan-American Copyright Conventions. Published
in the United States by Random House Children's Books, a division of Random House, Inc.,
New York, and simultaneously in Canada by Random House of Canada Limited, Toronto.

www.stepintoreading.com
www.thomasthetankengine.com

Educators and librarians, for a variety of teaching tools, visit us at
www.randomhouse.com/teachers

Library of Congress Cataloging-in-Publication Data
Awdry, W.
The great race / based on The Railway Series by the Rev. W. Awdry ; illustrated by Tom
LaPadula and Eric Binder. p. cm. — (Step into reading. A step 1 book)
SUMMARY: Thomas the tank engine and Bertie the bus agree to race to see who is faster.
ISBN 0-375-80284-3 (trade) — ISBN 0-375-90284-8 (lib. bdg.)
[1. Railroads—Trains—Fiction. 2. Buses—Fiction. 3. Racing—Fiction.]
I. LaPadula, Tom, ill. II. Binder, Eric, ill. III. Title. IV. Series: Step into reading. Step 1 book.
PZ7.A9613 Gr 2003 [E]—dc21 2002152415

Printed in the United States of America 30 29 28 27 26 25 24

STEP INTO READING, RANDOM HOUSE, and the Random House colophon are registered trademarks
of Random House, Inc.

THE GREAT RACE

Based on *The Railway Series*
by the Rev. W. Awdry

Illustrated by Tom LaPadula
and Eric Binder

Random House 🏠 New York

Thomas is a tank engine.

Bertie is a bus.

"I can go faster

than you,"

says Thomas.

"I will race you,"

Bertie says.

Off they go!

Thomas rides on tracks.

Clack-clack!

Clack-clack!

Bertie drives on roads.

Thomas pulls Annie
and Clarabel.

"Go fast!" they call.

"Go faster!"

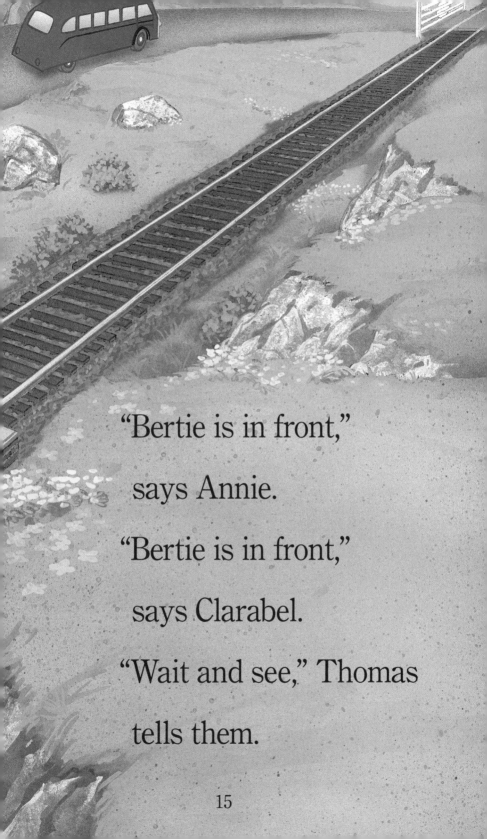

"Bertie is in front,"

says Annie.

"Bertie is in front,"

says Clarabel.

"Wait and see," Thomas

tells them.

The road crosses

the tracks.

Bertie has to stop.

"Good-bye, Bertie,"

Thomas calls.

Now Thomas is in front.

But Thomas has to stop

to let the people off.

Bertie catches up!

"Good-bye, Thomas,"
Bertie says.

Now Bertie is in front.

"Go fast," says Annie.

"Go faster," says Clarabel.

"Wait and see," Thomas

tells them.

A hill is up ahead.

Bertie takes the road around.

Thomas takes a tunnel straight

through the hill.

Thomas wins the race!

"That was fun," says Bertie.

"Peep, peep,"

says Thomas.

"Yes, it was."